HORRiD HENRY
AND THE
SOCCER FiEND

Meet HORRiD HENRY
the laugh-out-loud
worldwide sensation!

....

* Over 15 million copies sold in 27 countries and counting

* # 1 chapter book series in the UK

* Francesca Simon is the only American author to ever win the Galaxy British Book Awards Children's Book of the year (past winners include J.K. Rowling, Philip Pullman, and Eoin Colfer).

"Horrid Henry is a fabulous antihero...**a modern comic classic**." —*Guardian*

"**Wonderfully appealing to girls and boys alike**, a precious rarity at this age." —Judith Woods, *Times*

....

"The best children's comic writer." —Amanda Craig, *Times*

....

"**I love the Horrid Henry books by Francesca Simon**. They have lots of funny bits in. And Henry always gets into trouble!" —Mia, age 6, *BBC Learning Is Fun*

"My two boys love this book, and **I have actually had tears running down my face and had to stop reading because of laughing so hard**." —T. Franklin, Parent

"**It's easy to see why Horrid Henry is the bestselling character for five- to eight-year-olds**." —*Liverpool Echo*

"Francesca Simon's truly horrific little boy is **a monstrously enjoyable creation**. Parents love them because Henry makes their own little darlings seem like angels." —*Guardian Children's Books Supplement*

"I have tried out the Horrid Henry books with groups of children as a parent, as a babysitter, and as a teacher. **Children love to either hear them read aloud or to read them themselves**." —Danielle Hall, Teacher

"A flicker of recognition must pass through most teachers and parents when they read Horrid Henry. **There's a tiny bit of him in all of us**." —Nancy Astee, *Child Education*

"**As a teacher...it's great to get a series of books my class loves**. They go mad for Horrid Henry." —A teacher

"**Henry is a beguiling hero who has entranced millions of reluctant readers**." —*Herald*

....

"An absolutely fantastic series and surely a winner with all children. Long live Francesca Simon and her brilliant books! More, more please!"   —A parent

....

"**Laugh-out-loud reading for both adults and children alike**." —A parent

"**Horrid Henry certainly lives up to his name, and his antics are everything you hope your own child will avoid—which is precisely why younger children so enjoy these tales**." —*Independent on Sunday*

"Henry might be unbelievably naughty, totally wicked, and utterly horrid, but **he is frequently credited with converting the most reluctant readers into enthusiastic ones**...superb in its simplicity." —*Liverpool Echo*

Horrid Henry by Francesca Simon

Horrid Henry

Horrid Henry Tricks the Tooth Fairy

Horrid Henry and the Mega-Mean Time Machine

Horrid Henry's Stinkbomb

Horrid Henry and the Mummy's Curse

Horrid Henry and the Soccer Fiend

Horrid Henry Tricks and Treats

Horrid Henry's Christmas

HORRID HENRY
AND THE
SOCCER FIEND

Francesca Simon
Illustrated by Tony Ross

SOURCEBOOKS
Jabberwocky
AN IMPRINT OF SOURCEBOOKS

visit us at www.abdopublishing.com

Reinforced library bound edition published in 2013 by Spotlight, a
division of the ABDO Group, PO Box 398166, Minneapolis, MN 55439.
Spotlight produces high-quality reinforced library bound editions for
schools and libraries. Published by agreement with Sourcebooks, Inc.

Printed in the United States of America, North Mankato, Minnesota.
042012
092012

*To Elaine and Mark Eisenthal,
and to Alexander, Josh, and Katherine*

Library of Congress Cataloging-in-Publication Data

This book was previously cataloged with the following information:
Simon, Francesca.
  [Horrid Henry and the football fiend]
  Horrid Henry and the soccer fiend / Francesca Simon ; illustrated by Tony Ross.
    p. cm.
  [1. Behavior—Fiction. 2. Humorous stories.] I. Ross, Tony, ill. II. Title.
  PZ7.S604Hoaw 2009
  [Fic]—dc22
                          2008039689
ISBN 978-1-59961-189-1 (reinforced library edition)

All Spotlight books are reinforced library bindings
and manufactured in the United States of America.

CONTENTS

1

HORRID HENRY PEEKS AT PETER'S DIARY

"What are you doing?" demanded Horrid Henry, bursting into Peter's bedroom.

"Nothing," said Perfect Peter quickly, slamming his notebook shut.

"Yes you are," said Henry.

"Get out of my room," said Peter. "You're not allowed to come in unless I say so."

Horrid Henry leaned over Peter's shoulder.

"What are you writing?"

"None of your business," said Peter.

He covered the closed notebook tightly with his arm.

"It is *too* my business if you're writing about *me*."

"It's *my* diary. I can write what I want to," said Peter. "Miss Lovely said we should keep a diary for a week and write in it every day."

"Bo-ring," said Henry, yawning.

"No it isn't," said Peter. "Anyway, you'll find out next week what I'm writing: I've been chosen to read my diary out loud for our class assembly."

Horrid Henry's heart turned to ice.

Peter read his diary out loud? So the whole school could hear Peter's lies about him? No way!

"Gimme that!" screamed Horrid Henry, lunging for the diary.

"No!" screamed Peter, holding on tight. "MOOOM! Help! Henry's in my room!

And he didn't knock! And he won't leave!"

"Shut up, tattletale," hissed Henry, forcing Peter's fingers off the diary.

"MOOOOMMMMMM!" shrieked Peter.

Mom stomped up the stairs.

Henry opened the diary. But before he could read a single word Mom burst in.

"He snatched my diary! And he told me to shut up!" wailed Peter.

"Henry! Stop annoying your brother," said Mom.

"I wasn't," said Henry.

3

"Yes he was," sniveled Peter.

"And now you've made him cry," said Mom. "Say sorry."

"I was just asking about his homework," protested Henry innocently.

"He was trying to read my diary," said Peter.

"Henry!" said Mom. "Don't be horrid. A diary is private. Now leave your brother alone."

It was so unfair. Why did Mom always believe Peter?

Humph. Horrid Henry stalked out of Peter's bedroom. Well, no way was Henry waiting until the class assembly to find out what Peter had written.

Sneak. Sneak. Sneak.

Horrid Henry checked to the right. Horrid Henry checked to the left. Mom was downstairs working on the computer.

Dad was in the garden. Peter was playing at Goody-Goody Gordon's house.

At last, the coast was clear. He'd been trying to get ahold of Peter's diary for days. There was no time to lose.

Tomorrow was Peter's class assembly. Would he mention Sunday's food fight, when Henry had been forced to throw soggy pasta at Peter? Or when Henry had to push Peter off the comfy black chair and pinch him? Or yesterday when Henry banished him from the

 Purple
Hand
Club
and
Peter had
run screaming
to Mom? A lying,
slimy worm like Peter would be sure to
make it look like Henry was the villain
when in fact Peter was always to blame.

Even worse, what horrid lies had
Peter been making up about him?
People would read Peter's ravings and
think they were true. When Henry was
famous, books would be written about
him, and someone would find Peter's
diary and believe it! When things were
written down they had a horrible way
of seeming to be true even when they
were big fat lies.

Henry sneaked into Peter's bedroom

and shut the door. Now, where was that diary? Henry glanced at Peter's tidy desk. Peter kept it on the second shelf, next to his crayons and trophies.

The diary was gone.

Rats. Peter must have hidden it.

That little worm, thought Horrid Henry. Why on earth would he hide his diary? And *where* on earth would that smelly toad hide it? Behind his "Good as Gold" certificates? In the laundry basket? Underneath his stamp collection?

He checked Peter's sock drawer. No diary.

He checked Peter's underwear drawer. No diary.

He peeked under Peter's pillow, and under Peter's bed.

Still no diary.

OK, where would *I* hide a diary, thought Horrid Henry desperately. Easy. I'd put it in a chest and bury it in the garden, with a pirate curse on it.

Somehow he doubted Perfect Peter  would be so clever.

OK, thought Henry, if I were an ugly toad like him, where would I hide it?

The bookcase. Of course. What better place to hide a book?

Henry strolled over to Peter's book-case, with all the books arranged neatly in alphabetical order. Aha! What was

that sticking out between *The Happy Nappy* and *The Hoppy Hippo*?

Gotcha, thought Horrid Henry, yanking the diary off the shelf. At last he would know Peter's secrets. He'd make him cross out all his lies if it was the last thing he did.

Horrid Henry sat down and began to read:

<u>Monday</u>
Today I drew a picture of my teacher,
Miss Lovely. Miss Lovely gave me a
gold star for reading. That's because
I'm the best reader in the class. And
the best at math. And the best at
everything else.

<u>Tuesday</u>
Today I said please and thank you
236 times

<u>Wednesday</u>
Today I ate all my vegetables

Thursday
Today I sharpened my pencils.
I ate all my sprouts and had
Seconds.

Friday
Today I wrote a poem to my mom
    I Love my mom
    I want to wave a pom-pom
    I came out of her tummy,
    Her food is yummy,
    I love my mom.

Slowly Horrid Henry closed Peter's
diary. He knew Peter's diary would be
bad. But never in his worst nightmares
had he imagined anything this bad.

Perfect Peter hadn't mentioned him
once. Not once.

You'd think I didn't even live in this
house, thought Henry. He was outraged.

How dare Peter *not* write about him? And then all the stupid things Peter *had* written.

Henry's name would be mud when people heard Peter's diary in the assembly and found out what a sad brother he had. Everyone would tease him. Horrid Henry would never live down the shame.

Peter needed Henry's help, and he needed it fast. Horrid Henry grabbed a pencil and got to work.

Monday
Today I drew a picture of my teacher,
Miss Lovely. I drew her with piggy
ears and a grate big giant belly
Then I turned it into a
dartbord. Miss Lovely gave me
a gold star for reading. Miss
Lovely is my worst teecher
ever. She should reely be
called Miss Lumpy.
Miss Dumpy Lumpy is wot Gordon
and I call her behind her back.
Tee hee, she'll never know!

I'm the best reader in the class. And

the best at math. And the best at
everything else. Too bad I have
smelly pants and dirty hair

That's more like it, thought Horrid
Henry.

Tuesday
Today I said please and thank you
236 times

Not! I called Mom a big
blobby pants face. I called Dad
a stinky fish. Then I played
Pirats with the worlds greatest
brother, Henry. I Wish I were as
smart as Henry. But I know
thats imposibel.

Wednesday
Today I ate all my vegetables

then I sneaked tons of candy from the candy Jar and lied to dad about it. I am a very good liar. No one should ever beleeve a word I say. Henry gets the blame but reely every thing is always my fault.

Thursday
Today I sharpened my pencils.
All the better to write rude notes!
I ate all my sprouts and had seconds. Then threw up all over Mom. Eeugh, what a smell. I reelly am a smelly toad. I am so lucky to have a grate brother like Henry. He is always so nice to me Hip Hip Hurray for Henry

Friday
Today I wrote a poem to my bottom
   I Love my bottom
   I want to wave a pom-pom
   I love my bottom

Much better, thought Horrid Henry. Now that's what I call a diary. Everyone would have died of boredom otherwise.

Henry carefully replaced Peter's diary in the bookcase. I hope Peter appreciates what I've done for him, thought Horrid Henry.

The entire school gathered in the hall for the assembly. Peter's class sat proudly on benches at the front. Henry's class sat cross-legged on the floor. The parents sat on chairs down both sides.

Mom and Dad waved at Peter. He waved shyly back.

Miss Lovely stood up.

"Hello moms and dads, boys and girls, welcome to our class assembly. This quarter our class has been keeping diaries. We're going to read some of them to you now. First to read will be Peter. Everyone pay attention, and see if you too can be as good as I know Peter has been. I'd like everyone here to copy one of Peter's good deeds. I know I can't wait to hear how he has spent this last week."

Peter stood up, and opened his diary. In a big loud voice, he read:

"MONDAY:

"Today I drew a picture of my teacher, Miss Lovely."

Peter glanced up at Miss Lovely. She beamed at him.

"I drew her with piggy ears and a great big giant belly. Then I turned it into a dartboard."

What??! It was always difficult to read out loud and understand what he had read, but something didn't sound right. He didn't remember writing about a pig with a big belly. Nervously Peter looked up at Mom and Dad. Was he imagining it, or did their smiles seem more like frowns? Peter shook his head, and carried on.

"Miss Lovely gave me a gold star for reading."

Phew, that was better! He must have misheard himself before.

"Miss Lovely is my worst teacher ever. She should really be called Miss Lumpy. Miss Dumpy Lumpy—"

"Thank you, that's quite enough," interrupted Miss Lovely sternly, as the school erupted in shrieks of laughter. Her face was pink. "Peter, see me after the assembly. Ted will now tell us all about skeletons."

"But—but—" gasped Perfect Peter. "I—I didn't, I never—"

"Sit down and be quiet," said the principal, Mrs. Oddbod. "I'll see you *and* your parents later."

"WAAAAAAAAAA!" wailed Peter.

Mom and Dad stared at their feet. Why had they ever had children? Where was a trap door when you needed one?

"Waaaaaaaa," whimpered Mom and Dad.

Naturally, Henry got into trouble. Big, big trouble. It was so unfair. Why didn't anyone believe him when he said he'd improved Peter's diary for his own good? Honestly, he would never *ever* do Peter a favor again.

2

HORRID HENRY
AND THE
SOCCER FIEND

". . . AND with 15 seconds to go it's
Hot-Foot Henry racing across the field!
Beckham tries a slide tackle but Henry's
too quick! Just look at that step-over!
Oh no, he can't score from that distance,
it's crazy, it's impossible, oh my good-
ness, he cornered the ball, it's IN!!!! It's
IN! Another *spectacular* goal! Another
spectacular win! And it's all thanks to
Hot-Foot Henry, the greatest soccer star
who's ever lived!"

"Goal! Goal! Goal!" roared the crowd. Hot-Foot Henry won the match! His teammates carried him through the fans, cheering and chanting, "Hen-ry! Hen-ry! Hen-ry!"

"HENRY!"

Horrid Henry looked up to see Miss Battle-Axe leaning over his table and glaring at him with her red eyes.

"What did I just say?"

"Henry," said Horrid Henry.

Miss Battle-Axe scowled.

"I'm watching you, Henry," she snapped. "Now class, please pay attention, we need to discuss—"

 "Waaaaa!" wailed Weepy William.

"Susan, stop pulling my hair!" squealed Vain Violet.

24

"Miss!" shouted Inky Ian, "Ralph snatched my pen!"

"Did not!" shouted Rude Ralph.

"Did too!" shouted Inky Ian.

"Class! Be quiet!" bellowed Miss Battle-Axe.

"Waaaaa!" wailed Weepy William.

"Owwww!" squealed Vain Violet.

"Give it back!" shouted Inky Ian.

"Fine," said Miss Battle-Axe, "we won't talk about soccer."

William stopped wailing.

Violet stopped squealing.

Ian stopped shouting.

Henry stopped daydreaming.

Everyone in the class stared at Miss Battle-Axe. Miss Battle-Axe wanted to talk about…soccer? Was this an alien Miss Battle-Axe?

"As you all know, our local team, Ashton Athletic, has reached the sixth round of the National Soccer Cup," said Miss Battle-Axe.

"YAY!" shrieked the class.

"And I'm sure you all know what happened last night…"

Last night! Henry could still hear the announcer's glorious words as he and Peter had gathered around the radio as the draw for round six was announced.

"Number 16, Ashton Athletic, will be playing..." there was a long pause as the announcer drew another ball from the hat..."number 7, Manhattan United."

"Go Ashton!" shrieked Horrid Henry.

"As I was saying, before I was so rudely interrupted—" Miss Battle-Axe glared at Horrid Henry, "Ashton are playing Manhattan United in a few weeks. Every local elementary school has been given a pair of tickets. And thanks to my good luck in the teacher's draw, the lucky winner will come from our class."

"Me!" screamed Horrid Henry.

"Me!" screamed Moody Margaret.

27

"Me!" screamed Tough Toby, Aerobic Al, Fiery Fiona, and Brainy Brian.

"No one who shouts out will be getting anything," said Miss Battle-Axe. "Our class will be playing a soccer match at lunchtime. The best player of the match will win the tickets. I'm the referee and my decision will be final."

Horrid Henry was so stunned that for a moment he could scarcely breathe. National Soccer Cup tickets! National Soccer Cup tickets to see his local team Ashton play against Man U! Those tickets were like gold dust. Henry had begged and pleaded with Mom and

Dad to get tickets, but naturally they were all sold out by the time Henry's mean, horrible, lazy parents managed to heave their stupid bones to the phone. And now here was another chance to go to the match of the century!

Ashton Athletic had never got so far in the Cup. Sure, they'd knocked out the Tooting Tigers (chant: Toot Toot! Grrr!) the Pynchley Pythons and the Cheam Champions but—Manhattan United! Henry had to go to the game. He just had to. And all he had to do was be MVP.

There was just one problem. Unfortunately, the best soccer player in the class wasn't Horrid Henry. Or Aerobic Al. Or Beefy Bert.

The best soccer player in the class was Moody Margaret. The second best player in the class was Moody Margaret.

The third best player in the class was
Moody Margaret. It was so unfair! Why
should Margaret of all people be so
fantastic at soccer?

Horrid Henry was great at shirt
pulling. Horrid Henry was superb at

screaming "Offside!" (whatever that meant). No one could howl "Come on, ref!" louder. And at toe treading, elbowing, barging, pushing, shoving, and tripping, Horrid Henry had no equal. The only thing Horrid Henry wasn't good at was playing soccer.

But never mind. Today would be different. Today he would dig deep inside and find the power to be Hot-Foot Henry—for real. Today no one would stop him. National Soccer Cup match here I come, thought Horrid Henry gleefully.

Lunchtime!

Horrid Henry's class dashed to the back playground, where the field was set up. Two sweatshirts either end marked the goals. A few parents gathered on the sidelines.

Miss Battle-Axe split the class into two teams: Aerobic Al was captain of Henry's team, Moody Margaret was captain of the other.

There she stood in midfield, having nabbed a striker position, smirking confidently. Horrid Henry glared at her from the depths of the outfield.

"Na na ne nah nah, I'm sure to be MVP," trilled Moody Margaret, sticking out her tongue at him. "And you-ooo won't."

"Shut up, Margaret," said Henry. When he was king, anyone named Margaret would be boiled in oil and fed to the crows.

"Will you take me to the match, Margaret?" said Susan. "After all, *I'm* your best friend."

Moody Margaret scowled. "Since when?"

"Since always!" wailed Susan.

"Huh!" said Margaret. "We'll just have to see how nice you are to me, won't we?"

"Take me," begged Brainy Brian. "Remember how I helped you with those fractions?"

"And called me stupid," said Margaret.

"Did not," said Brian.

"Did too," said Margaret.

Horrid Henry eyed his classmates. Everyone looking straight ahead, everyone determined to be MVP. Well, wouldn't they be in for a shock when Horrid Henry waltzed off with those tickets!

"Go Margaret!" screeched Moody Margaret's mom.

"Go Al!" screeched Aerobic Al's dad.

"Everyone ready?" said Miss Battle-Axe. "Bert! Which team are you on?"

"I dunno," said Beefy Bert.

Miss Battle-Axe blew her whistle.

Kick-off!

Kick.

 Chase.

Kick.

Dribble.

Dribble.

Pass.

Kick,

Save!

 Goal Kick

Henry stood disconsolately on the left wing, running back and forth as the play passed him by. How could he ever be MVP stuck out here? Well, no way was he staying in this stupid spot a moment longer.

Horrid Henry abandoned his position and chased after the ball. All the other defenders followed him.

Moody Margaret had the ball. Horrid Henry ran up behind her. He glanced at Miss Battle-Axe. She was busy chatting to Mrs. Oddbod. Horrid Henry went for a two-foot slide tackle and tripped her.

"Foul!" screeched Margaret. "He hacked my leg!"

"Liar!" screeched Henry. "I just went for the ball!"

"Cheater!" screamed Moody Margaret's mom.

"Play on," ordered Miss Battle-Axe.

Yes! thought Horrid Henry trium-
phantly. After all, what did blind old
Miss Battle-Axe know about the rules
of soccer? Nothing. This was his golden
chance to score.

Now Jazzy Jim had the ball.

Horrid Henry
stepped on his
toes, elbowed
him, and grabbed
the ball.

"Hey,
we're on
the same
team!"
yelped Jim.

Horrid Henry kept dribbling.

"Pass! Pass!" screamed Al. "I'm open!"

Henry ignored him. Pass the ball? Was
Al crazy? For once Henry had the ball
and he was keeping it.

Then suddenly Moody Margaret appeared from behind, barged him, dribbled the ball past Henry's team, and kicked it straight past Weepy William into the goal. Moody Margaret's team cheered.

Weepy William burst into tears.

"Waaaaaa," wailed Weepy William.

"Idiot!" screamed Aerobic Al's dad.

"She cheated!" shrieked Henry. "She fouled me!"

"Didn't," said Margaret.

"How dare you call my daughter a cheater?" screamed Margaret's mom.

Miss Battle-Axe blew her whistle.

"Goal to Margaret's team. The score is one—nothing."

Horrid Henry gritted his teeth. He would score a goal if he had to trample on every player to do so.

Unfortunately, everyone else seemed to have the same idea.

"Ralph pushed me!" shrieked Aerobic Al.

"Didn't!" lied Rude Ralph. "It was just an accident."

"He used his hands; I saw him!" howled Al's father. "Send him off."

"I'll send *you* off if you don't behave," snapped Miss Battle-Axe, looking up and blowing her whistle.

"It was kept in!" protested Henry.

"No way!" shouted Margaret. "It went past the line!"

"That was ball to hand!" yelled Kind Kasim.

"No way!" screamed Aerobic Al. "I just went for the ball."

"Liar!"

"Liar!"

"Free kick to Margaret's team," said Miss Battle-Axe.

"Ouch!" screamed Soraya, as Brian stepped on her toes, grabbed the ball, and headed it into the goal past Kasim.

"Hurray!" cheered Al's team.

"Foul!" screamed Margaret's team.

"Score is one all," said Miss Battle-Axe. "Five more minutes to go."

AAARRRGGHH! thought Horrid Henry. I've got to score a goal to have a chance to be MVP. I've just got to. But how, how?

Henry glanced at Miss Battle-Axe. She appeared to be rummaging in her purse. Henry saw his chance. He stuck out his foot as Margaret hurtled past.

Crash!

Margaret tumbled.

Henry seized the ball.

"Henry kicked my leg!" shrieked Margaret.

"Did not!" shrieked Henry. "I just went for the ball."

"REF!" screamed Margaret.

"He cheated!" screamed Margaret's mom. "Are you blind, ref?"

Miss Battle-Axe glared.

"My eyesight is perfect, thank you," she snapped.

Tee hee, chortled Horrid Henry.

Henry stepped on Brian's toes, elbowed him, then grabbed the ball. Then Dave elbowed Henry, Ralph trod on Dave's toes, and Susan seized the ball and kicked it high overhead.

Henry looked up. The ball was high, high up. He'd never reach it, not unless, unless—Henry glanced at Miss Battle-Axe. She was watching a traffic officer patrolling outside the school gate. Henry leapt into the air and whacked the ball with his hand.

Thwack!

The ball hurled across the goal.

"Goal!" screamed Henry.

"He used his hands!" protested Margaret.

"No way!" shouted Henry. "It was the hand of God!"

"Henry! Henry! Hen-ry!" cheered his team.

"Unfair!" howled Margaret's team.

Miss Battle-Axe blew her whistle.

"Time!" she bellowed. "Al's team wins 2–1."

"Yes!" shrieked Horrid Henry, punching the air. He'd scored the winning goal! He'd be MVP! Ashton Athletic versus Man U, here I come!

★ ★ ★

Horrid Henry's class limped through the door and sat down. Horrid Henry sat at the front, beaming. Miss Battle-Axe had to award him the tickets after his brilliant performance and spectacular, game-winning goal. The question was, who *deserved* to be his guest?

No one.

I know, thought Horrid Henry, I'll sell my other ticket. Bet I get a million dollars for it. No, a billion dollars. Then I'll buy my own team, and play striker any time I want to. Horrid Henry smiled happily.

Miss Battle-Axe glared at her class.

"That was absolutely disgraceful," she said. "Cheating! Moving the goals!

Shirt tugging!" she glared at Graham.
"Pushing!"

She glowered at Ralph. "Pushing and
shoving! Bad sportsmanship!" Her eyes
swept over the class.

Horrid Henry sank lower in his seat.
Oops.

"And don't get me started about the
offsides penalties," she snapped.

Horrid Henry sank even lower.

"There was only one person who
deserves to be MVP," she continued.
"One person who observed the rules
of the beautiful game. One person who
has nothing to be ashamed of today."

Horrid Henry's heart leapt. *He*
certainly had nothing to be ashamed of.

"... One person who can
truly be proud of his or
her performance ..."

Horrid Henry beamed with pride.

"And that person is—"

"Me!" screamed Moody Margaret.

"Me!" screamed Aerobic Al.

"Me!" screamed Horrid Henry.

"—the referee," said Miss Battle-Axe.

What?

Miss Battle-Axe…MVP?

Miss Battle-Axe…a soccer fiend?

"IT's NOT FAIR!" screamed the class.

"IT's NOT FAIR!" screamed Horrid Henry.

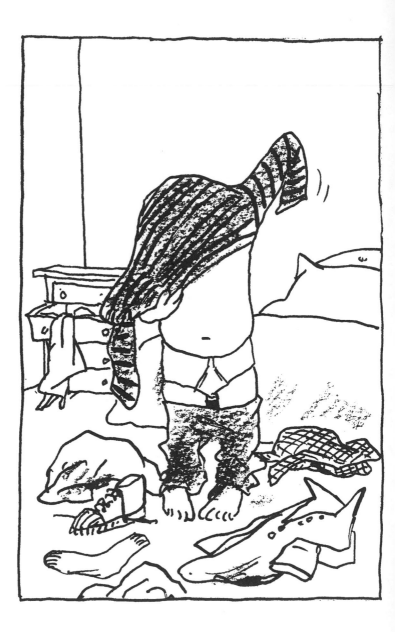

3

....

HORRID HENRY
GOES SHOPPING

Horrid Henry stood in his bedroom up
to his knees in clothes. The long sleeve
stripy T-shirt came to his elbow. His
pants stopped halfway down his legs.
Henry sucked in his tummy as hard as
he could. Still the zipper wouldn't zip.

"Nothing fits!" he screamed, yanking off
the shirt and hurling it across the room.
"And my shoes hurt."

"All right, Henry, calm down," said
Mom. "You've grown. We'll go out
this afternoon and get you some new
clothes and shoes."

"NOOOOOOO!" shrieked Henry.
"NOOOOOOOOOOOOO!"

Horrid Henry hated shopping.

Correction: Horrid Henry loved shopping. He loved shopping for gigantic TVs, computer games, comics, toys, and candy. Yet for some reason Horrid Henry's parents never wanted to go shopping for good stuff. Oh no. They shopped for vacuum bags. Toothpaste. Spinach. Socks. Why oh why did he have such horrible parents? When he was grown up he'd never set foot in a supermarket. He'd only shop for TVs, computer games, and chocolate.

But shopping for clothes was even worse than heaving his heavy bones around the Happy Shopper Supermarket. Nothing was more boring than being dragged around miles and miles and miles of shops, filled with disgusting clothes only a mutant would ever want to wear, and then standing in a little room while Mom made you try on icky scratchy things you wouldn't be seen dead in if they were the last pair of pants on earth. It was horrible enough getting dressed once a day without doing it fifty times. Just thinking about trying on shirt after shirt after shirt made Horrid Henry want to scream.

"I'm not going shopping!" he howled, kicking the pile of clothes as viciously as he could. "And you can't make me."

"What's all this yelling?" demanded Dad.

"Henry needs new pants," said Mom grimly.

Dad went pale.

"Are you sure?"

"Yes," said Mom. "Take a look at him."

Dad looked at Henry. Henry scowled.

"They're a *little* small, but not *that* bad," said Dad.

"I can't breathe in these pants!" shrieked Henry.

"That's why we're going shopping,"

said Mom. "And *I'll* take him." Last
time Dad had taken Henry shopping for
socks and came back instead with three
Hairy Hellhound CDs and a jumbo
pack of Day-Glo slime.

"I don't know what came over me,"
Dad had said when Mom told him off.

"But why do *I* have to go?" said Henry.
"I don't want to waste my precious time
shopping."

"What about *my* precious time?"
said Mom.

Henry scowled. Parents didn't have
precious time. They were there to serve
their children. New pants should just
magically appear, like clean clothes and
packed lunches.

Mom's face brightened. "Wait, I have
an idea," she beamed. She rushed out
and came back with a large plastic bag.
"Here," she said, pulling out a pair of

bright red pants, "try
these on."

Henry looked at them
suspiciously.

"Where are they
from?"

"Aunt Ruby dropped off
some of Steve's old clothes
a few weeks ago. I'm sure
we'll find something that
fits you."

Horrid Henry stared at Mom. Had
she gone gaga? Was she actually sug-
gesting that he should wear his horrible cousin's moldy old shirts and
smelly pants? Just imagine, putting his
arms into the same stinky sleeves that
Stuck-up Steve had slimed? Uggh!

"NO WAY!" screamed Henry, shuddering. "I'm not wearing Steve's smelly
old clothes. I'd catch rabies."

"They're practically brand new," said Mom.

"I don't care," said Henry.

"But Henry," said Perfect Peter. "I always wear *your* hand-me-downs."

"So?" snarled Henry.

"I don't mind wearing hand-me-downs," said Perfect Peter. "It saves so much money. You shouldn't be so self-ish, Henry."

"Quite right, Peter," said Mom, smiling. "At least *one* of my sons thinks about others."

Horrid Henry pounced. He was a vampire sampling his supper.

"AAIIIEEEEEE!" squealed Peter.

"Stop that, Henry!" screamed Mom.

"Leave your brother alone!" screamed Dad.

Horrid Henry glared at Peter.

"Peter is a worm, Peter is a toad," jeered Henry.

"Mom!" wailed Peter. "Henry said I was a worm. And a toad."

"Don't be horrid, Henry," said Dad. "Or no TV for a week. You have three choices. Wear Steve's old clothes. Wear your old clothes. Go shopping for new ones today."

"Do we *have* to go today?" moaned Henry.

"Fine," said Mom. "We'll go tomorrow."

"I don't want to go tomorrow," wailed Henry. "My weekend will be ruined."

Mom glared at Henry.

"Then we'll go right now this minute."

"NO!" screamed Horrid Henry.

"YES!" screamed Mom.

★ ★ ★

Several hours later, Mom and Henry
walked into Mellow Mall. Mom already
looked like she'd been crossing the
Sahara desert
without water
for days. Serves
her right for
bringing me
here, thought
Horrid Henry,
scowling,
as he scuffed his
feet.

"Can't we go
to Shop 'n' Drop?" whined Henry.
"Graham says they've got a win your
weight in chocolate competition."

"No," said Mom, dragging Henry
into Zippy's Department Store. "We're
here to get you some new pants and shoes.
Now hurry up, we don't have all day."

Horrid Henry looked around. Wow! There was lots of great stuff on display.

"I want the Hip-Hop Robots," said Henry.

"No," said Mom.

"I want the new Waterblaster!" screeched Henry.

"No," said Mom.

"I want a Creepy Crawly lunch box!"

"NO!" said Mom, pulling him into the boys' clothing department.

What, thought Horrid Henry grimly, is the point of going shopping if you never buy anything?

"I want Root-a-Toot sneakers with flashing red lights," said Henry. He could see himself now, strolling into class, a bugle blasting and red light flashing every time his feet hit the floor. Cool! He'd love to see Miss Battle-Axe's face when he exploded into class wearing them.

"No," said Mom, shuddering.

"Oh please," said Henry.

"NO!" said Mom, "We're here to buy pants and sensible school shoes."

"But I want Root-a-Toot sneakers!" screamed Horrid Henry. "Why can't we buy what *I* want to buy? You're the meanest mother in the world and I hate you!"

"Don't be horrid, Henry. Go and try these on," said Mom, grabbing a selection of hideous pants and revolting T-shirts. "I'll keep looking."

Horrid Henry sighed loudly and slumped toward the dressing room. No one in the world suffered as much as he did. Maybe he could hide between the clothes racks and never come out.

Then something wonderful in the toy department next door caught his eye.

Whooa! A whole row of the new megalotronic animobotic robots with 213 programmable actions. Horrid Henry dumped the clothes and ran over to have a look. Oooh, the new Intergalactic Samurai Gorillas that launched real stinkbombs! And the latest Waterblasters! And deluxe Dungeon Drink kits with a celebrity chef recipe book! To say nothing of the Mega-Whirl Goo Shooter that sprayed fluorescent goo for fifty yards in every direction. Wow!

Mom staggered into the dressing room with more clothes. "Henry?" said Mom.

No reply.

"HENRY!" said Mom.

Still no reply.

Mom yanked open a dressing room door.

"Hen—"

"Excuse *me!*" yelped a bald man, standing in his underpants.

"Sorry," said Mom, blushing bright pink. She dashed out of the changing room and scanned the shop floor.

Henry was gone.

Mom searched up the aisles.

No Henry.

Mom searched down the aisles.

Still no Henry.

Then Mom saw a tuft of hair sticking up behind the neon sign for Ballistic Bazooka Boomerangs. She marched over and hauled Henry away.

"I was just looking," protested Henry.

Henry tried on one pair of pants after another.

"No, no, no, no, no, no, no," said Henry, kicking off the final pair. "I hate all of them."

"All right," said Mom, grimly. "We'll look somewhere else."

Mom and Henry went to Top Trousers. They went to Cool Clothes. They went to Stomp in the Swamp. Nothing had been right.

"Too tight," moaned Henry.

"Too itchy!"

68

"Too big!"

"Too small!"

"Too ugly!"

"Too red!"

"Too uncomfortable!"

"We're going to Tip-Top Togs," said Mom wearily. "The first thing that fits, we're buying."

Mom staggered into the children's department and grabbed a pair of pink and green plaid pants in Henry's size.

"Try these on," she ordered. "If they fit we're buying them."

Horrid Henry gazed in horror at the horrendous pants.

"Those are girls' pants!" he screamed.

"They are not," said Mom.

"Are too!" shrieked Henry.

"I'm sick and tired of your excuses, Henry," said Mom. "Put them on or no allowance for a year. I mean it."

Horrid Henry put on the pink and green plaid pants, puffing out his stomach as much as possible. Not even Mom would make him buy pants that were too tight.

Oh no. The horrible pants had an elastic waist. They would fit a mouse as easily as an elephant.

"And lots of room to grow," said Mom brightly. "You can wear them for years. Perfect."

"NOOOOOO!" howled Henry. He flung himself on the floor kicking and

screaming. "NOOOO! THEY'RE
GIRLS' PANTS!!!"

"We're buying them," said Mom. She
gathered up the plaid pants and stomped
over to the register. She tried not to
think about starting all over again trying
to find a pair of shoes that Henry would
wear.

A little girl in pigtails walked out of
the dressing room, twirling in pink and
green plaid pants.

"I love them, Mommy!" she shrieked.
"Let's get three pairs."

Horrid Henry stopped howling.

He looked at Mom.

Mom looked at Henry.

Then they both looked at the pink and green plaid pants Mom was carrying.

ROOT-A-TOOT!
ROOT-A-TOOT!
ROOT-A-TOOT!
TOOT! TOOT!

An earsplitting bugle blast shook the house. Flashing red lights bounced off the walls.

"What's that noise?" said Dad, covering his ears.

"What noise?" said Mom, pretending to read.

ROOT-A-TOOT!
ROOT-A-TOOT!

ROOT-A-TOOT! TOOT! TOOT!

Dad stared at Mom.

"You didn't," said Dad. "Not—Root-a-Toot sneakers?"

Mom hid her face in her hands.

"I don't know what came over me," said Mom.

4

HORRID HENRY'S ARCH ENEMY

"Be bop a lu la!" boomed Jazzy Jim, be-bopping around the class and bouncing to the beat.

"One day, my prince will come..." warbled Singing Soraya.

"Bam bam bam bam bam!" drummed Horrid Henry, crashing his books up and down on his table top.

"Class! Settle down!" shouted Miss Battle-Axe.

"Be bop a lu la!" boomed Jazzy Jim.

"One day, my prince will come..." warbled Singing Soraya.

"Bam bam bam bam bam!" drummed Horrid Henry.

"Jim!" barked Miss Battle-Axe. "Stop yowling. Soraya! Stop singing. Henry! Stop banging or everyone will miss playtime."

"Be bop—" faltered Jim.

"…Prince will—" squeaked Soraya.

"Bam bam bam bam bam," drummed Horrid Henry. He was Mad Moon Madison, crazy drummer for the Moldy

Drumsticks, whipping the shrieking crowd into a frenzy—

"HENRY!" bellowed Miss Battle-Axe. "STOP THAT NOISE!"

What did that ungrateful fan mean, noise? What noise? This wasn't noise, this was great music, this was—Mad Moon Madison looked up from his drum kit. Whoops.

Silence.

Miss Battle-Axe glared at her class. Oh, for the good old days,

 when teachers could whack horrible children with rulers.

"Linda! Stop snoring. Graham! Stop drooling. Bert! Where's your chair?"

"I dunno," said Beefy Bert.

There was a new boy standing next

to Miss Battle-Axe. His brown hair was tightly slicked back. His shoes were polished. He carried a trumpet and a calculator. Yuck! He looked like a complete idiot. Horrid Henry looked away. And then looked back. Funny, there was something familiar about that boy. The way he stood with his nose in the air. The horrid little smirk on his face. He

looked like—he looked just like—oh
no, please no, it couldn't be—Bossy
Bill! Bossy Bill!!

"Class, we have a new boy," said Miss
Battle-Axe, doing her best to twist her
thin lips into a welcoming smile. "I
need someone to look after him and
show him around. Who would like to
be Bill's friend for the day?"

Everyone put up their hand. Everyone but Horrid Henry. Uggh. Bossy
Bill. What kind of cruel joke was this?

79

Bossy Bill was the horrible, stuck-up son of Dad's boss. Horrid Henry hated Bill. Uggh! Yuck! Just thinking about Bill made Henry gag.

Henry had a suspicion he wasn't Bill's favorite person, either. The last time they'd met, Henry had tricked Bill into photocopying his bottom. Bill had got into trouble. Big, big trouble.

Miss Battle-Axe scanned the sea of waving hands.

"Me!" shouted Moody Margaret.

"Me!" shouted Kind Kasim.

"Me!" shouted Weepy William.

"There's an empty seat next to Henry," said Miss Battle-Axe, pointing. "Henry will look after you."

NO, thought Henry.

"Waaaaaa," wailed Weepy William. "I didn't get picked."

"Go and sit down, Bill," continued

Miss Battle-Axe. "Class, silent reading from page 12."

Bossy Bill walked between the tables toward Horrid Henry.

Maybe he won't recognize me, thought Henry hopefully. After all, it was a long time ago.

Suddenly Bill stopped. His face contorted with loathing.

Oops.

He recognized me, thought Horrid Henry.

Bill marched, scowling, to the seat next to Henry and sat down. His nose wrinkled as if he smelled a stinky smell.

"You say one word about what happened at my dad's office and I'll tell my dad," hissed Bill.

"You say one word to your dad and I'll tell everyone at school you photocopied your bottom," hissed Henry.

"Then I'll tell on you!"

"I'll tell on you!"

Bill shoved Henry.

Henry shoved Bill.

"He shoved me, Miss!" shouted Bossy
Bill.

"He shoved me first!" shouted Horrid
Henry.

"Henry!" said Miss Battle-Axe. "I am
shocked and appalled. Is this how you
welcome a new boy to our class?"

It is when the boy is Bossy Bill,
thought Henry grimly.

He glared at Bill.

Bill glared at Henry.

"My old school's a lot better than this dump," hissed Bossy Bill.

"So why don't you go back there?" hissed Henry. "No one's stopping you."

"Maybe I will," said Bill.

Horrid Henry's heart leapt. Was there a chance he could get Bill to leave?

"You don't want to stay here—we get four hours of homework a night," lied Henry.

"So?" said Bill. "My old school gave you five hours."

"The food's horrible."

"Big deal," said Bill.

"And Miss Battle-Axe is the meanest teacher in the world."

"What did you say, Henry?" demanded Miss Battle-Axe's ice cold dagger voice.

"I just told Bill you were the keenest teacher in the world," said Henry quickly.

"No he didn't," said Bill. "He said you were the meanest."

"Keenest," said Henry.

"Meanest," said Bill.

Miss Battle-Axe glared at Horrid Henry.

"I'm watching you, Henry. Now get back to work."

DING! DING! DING!

Hurray! Saved by the playtime bell.

Horrid Henry jumped from his seat. Maybe he could escape Bill if he ran out of class fast enough.

Henry pushed and shoved his way into the hall. Free! Free at last!

"Hey!" came an unwelcome voice beside him. A sweaty hand pulled on his shirt.

"The teacher said you're supposed to show me around," said Bossy Bill.

"OK, here are the bathrooms," snarled Horrid Henry, waving his hand in

the direction of the girls' bathroom. "And
the photocopier's in the office," he
added, pointing. "Why don't you try
it out?"

Bill scowled.

"I'm going to tell my dad that you at-
tacked me," said Bill. "In fact, I'm going
to tell my dad every single bad thing
you do in school. Then he'll tell yours
and you'll get into trouble. And won't I
laugh."

Henry's blood boiled. What had he
ever done to deserve Bossy Bill butting
into his life? A spy in his class. Could
school get any worse?

Aerobic Al jogged past.

"Henry photocopied his bottom at
my dad's office," said Bill loudly. "Boy,
did he get into trouble."

AAARRRGGHHH!

"That's a lie," said Horrid Henry hotly.

"Bill did, not me."

"Yeah right, Henry," said Dizzy Dave.

"Big bottom!" shrieked Moody Margaret.

"Big, big bottom!" shrieked Sour Susan. Bill smirked.

"Bye, big bottom," said Bill. "Don't forget, I'm watching you," he hissed.

Henry sat down by himself on the broken bench in the secret garden. He had to get Bill out of his class. School was horrible enough without someone evil like Bill spying on him and spreading nasty rumors. His life would be ruined. He had to get rid of Bill—fast. But how?

Maybe he could get Bill to run screaming from school and never come back. Wow, thought Horrid Henry. Wouldn't that be wonderful? Bye-bye Bossy Bill.

Or maybe he could get Bill to photocopy his bottom again. Probably not, thought Horrid Henry regretfully. Aha! He could trick Bill into dancing nude on Miss Battle-Axe's desk singing "I'm a busy bumblebee—buzz buzz buzz." That would be sure to get him expelled. The only trouble was—how?

I've got to think of something, thought Horrid Henry desperately. I've just got to.

★ ★ ★

"Henry," said Dad the next evening, "my boss tells me you've been picking on his son. Bill was very upset."

"He's picking on *me*," protested Henry.

"And that you were yelled at in class for shouting out."

"No way," lied Henry.

"And that you broke Andrew's pencil."

"That was an accident," said Henry.

"And that you called Margaret bug-face."

"I didn't," wailed Henry. "Bill's lying."

"I want you to be on your best behavior from now on," said Dad. "How do you think I feel hearing these reports about you from my boss? I've never been so embarrassed in my life."

"Who cares?" screamed Horrid Henry. "What about me?"

"Go to your room!" shouted Dad.

"FINE!" yelled Horrid Henry, slamming the door behind him as hard as he could. I'll beat you, Bill, thought Henry, if it's the last thing I do.

Horrid Henry tried teasing Bill.

Horrid Henry tried pinching Bill.

He tried spreading rumors about Bill.

He even tried getting Bill to punch him so Bill would be suspended.

But nothing worked. Henry just got into more and more trouble.

On Monday, Dad yelled at Henry for making rude noises in class.

On Tuesday, Dad yelled at Henry for talking during story time.

On Wednesday, Dad yelled at Henry for not handing in his homework.

On Thursday, Mom and Dad yelled at

Henry for chewing gum in class,
passing notes to Ralph, throwing food,
jiggling his desk, pulling
Margaret's hair, running down the hall,
and kicking a football into the back
playground. Then they banned him
from the computer for a week. And all
because of Bossy Bill.

★ ★ ★

Horrid Henry slunk into class. It was hopeless. Bill was here to stay. Horrid Henry would just have to grit his teeth and bear it.

Miss Battle-Axe started explaining electricity.

Henry looked around the classroom. Speaking of Bill, where was he?

Maybe he has rabies, thought Horrid Henry hopefully. Or fallen down the toilet. Better still, maybe he'd been kidnapped by aliens.

Or maybe he'd been expelled. Yes! Henry could see it now. Bill on his knees in Mrs. Oddbod's office,

begging to stay. Mrs. Oddbod pointing
to the door:

"Out of this school, you horrible
monster! How dare you spy on Henry,
our best pupil?"

"NOOO!" Bill would wail.

"BEGONE, WRETCH!" commanded
Mrs. Oddbod. And out went Bossy Bill,
sniveling, where armed
guards were waiting
to handcuff him and
take him to prison.
That must be
what had happened.

Henry smiled.
Oh joyful day!
No more
Bossy Bill,
thought
Horrid
Henry

happily, stretching his legs under his Bill-free table and taking a deep breath of Bill-free air.

"Henry!" snapped Miss Battle-Axe. "Come here."

What now?

Slowly Horrid Henry heaved himself out of his chair and scuffed his way to Miss Battle-Axe's desk, where she was busy slashing at homework with a bright red pen.

"Bill has a sore throat," said Miss Battle-Axe.

Rats, thought Horrid Henry. Where was the black plague when you needed it?

"His parents want him to have his homework assignments so he doesn't fall behind while he's sick," said Miss Battle-Axe. "If only *all* parents were so conscientious. Please give this math worksheet to your father to give to Bill's dad."

She handed Henry a piece of paper with ten multiplication sums on it and a large envelope.

"OK," said Henry dully. Not even the thought of Bill lying in bed doing sums could cheer him up. All too soon Bill would be back. He was stuck with Bill forever.

That night Horrid Henry glanced at Bill's

math worksheet. Ten sums. Not enough, really, he thought. Why should Bill be bored in bed with nothing to do but watch TV, and read comics, and eat chips?

And then Horrid Henry smiled. Bill wanted homework? Perhaps Henry could help. Tee hee, thought Horrid Henry, sitting down at the computer.

TAP.

TAP.

TAP.

HOMEWERK

Rite a storee abowt yor day. 20 pages long.

Ha ha ha, that will keep Bill busy, thought Horrid Henry. Now, what else? What else?

Aha!

Give ten reesons why watching TV is better than reading

NEW MATH
When does 2 + 2 =5 ?
When 2 is big enough.
Now explain why:
2+3=6
7-3=5

It was a lot more fun making up homework than doing it, thought Horrid Henry happily.

SPELLING:

Lern how to spel these words fer a test on Tuesday.

Terrantula

Stinkbomb

Moosli

Doovay

Screem

Intergalactik

SCEINSE

Gravity: does it work?

Drop an egg from a hight of 2 in. onto your mom or dad's hed.

***Record if it breaks. Drop an-
other egg from a hight of 4
in. onto yor carpet. Does this
egg break? Try this xperiment
at least 12 times all over yor house.***

Now that's what I call homework,
thought Horrid Henry. He printed out
the worksheets, popped them in the envelope with Miss Battle-Axe's sheet of
sums, sealed it, and gave it to Dad.

"Bill's homework,"
said Henry. "Miss
Battle-Axe asked me
to give it to you to
give to Bill's dad."

"I'll make sure he
gets it," said Dad, putting the envelope
in his briefcase. "I'm glad to see you're
becoming friends with Bill."

★ ★ ★

Dad looked stern.

"I've got some bad news for you, Henry," said Dad the next day.

Horrid Henry froze. What was he going to get told off about now? Oh no. Had Dad found out about what he'd done at lunchtime?

"I'm afraid Bill won't be coming back to your school," said Dad. "His parents have removed him. Something about new math and a gravity experiment that went wrong."

Horrid Henry's mouth opened. No sound came out.

"Wha—?" gasped Horrid Henry.

"Gravity experiment?" said Mom. "What gravity experiment?"

"Different science group," said Henry quickly.

"Oh," said Mom.

"Oh," said Dad.

A lovely warm feeling spread from Henry's head all the way down to his toes.

"So Bill's not coming back?"

"No," said Dad. "I'm sorry that you've lost a friend."

"I'll live," beamed Horrid Henry.

Acknowledgments

Special thanks to Freddy Gaminara and Michael Garner for telling me so many exciting ways to cheat at soccer.

About the Author

Photo: Francesco Guidicini

Francesca Simon spent her childhood on the beach in California and then went to Yale and Oxford Universities to study medieval history and literature. She now lives in London with her family. She has written over forty-five books and won the Children's Book of the Year in 2008 at the Galaxy British Book Awards for *Horrid Henry and the Abominable Snowman*.